A quick note from the creator of this book:

Thank you for purchasing this sketchbook/journal!
I find it very therapeutic to write and draw, and I hope you do too.
Sometimes creating an image from words can be challenging, but
I really want to encourage you to bring **your words to life.**

There is no right or wrong way to do this, and of course
only create it if you are comfortable with the subject and feel that it
will benefit you.

I hope you enjoy this book!
-*Dakota Daetwiler*

Write about anything you want..... Now sketch about what you wrote!

If you feel inclined, share on social media and tag me. I would
love to see your creations and interpretations!

www.PaintingsByDakota.com

Today's Date:

Today's Date:

Today's Date:

Today's Date:

Today's Date:

Today's Date:

Today's Date:

Today's Date:

Write from your heart

Today's Date:

Today's Date:

Today's Date:

Today's Date:

Today's Date:

Today's Date:

Today's Date:

Today's Date:

Today's Date:

Today's Date:

Today's Date:

Today's Date:

Today's Date:

Today's Date:

Today's Date:

Today's Date:

Today's Date:

Today's Date:

Today's Date:

Today's Date:

Today's Date:

Today's Date:

Today's Date:

Today's Date:

Today's Date:

Today's Date:

Today's Date:

Today's Date:

Today's Date:

Today's Date:

Today's Date:

Today's Date:

Today's Date:

Today's Date:

Today's Date:

Today's Date:

Today's Date:

Today's Date:

Today's Date:

Today's Date:

Today's Date:

Today's Date:

Today's Date:

Today's Date:

Today's Date:

Today's Date:

Today's Date:

Today's Date:

Today's Date:

Today's Date:

Today's Date:

Today's Date:

Today's Date:

Today's Date:

Today's Date:

Today's Date:

Today's Date:

Today's Date:

Today's Date:

Write from your heart

Today's Date:

Today's Date:

Today's Date:

Today's Date:

Today's Date:

Today's Date:

Today's Date:

Today's Date:

Today's Date:

Today's Date: _____

Today's Date:

Today's Date:

Write from your heart

Write from your heart

Today's Date:

Today's Date:

Today's Date:

Today's Date:

Today's Date:

Write from your heart

Today's Date:

Today's Date:

Today's Date:

Today's Date:

Write from your heart

Today's Date:

Today's Date:

Today's Date:

Today's Date:

Today's Date:

Today's Date:

Today's Date:

Today's Date:

Write from your heart

Today's Date:

Today's Date:

Today's Date:

Today's Date:

Today's Date:

Write from your heart ♥

Today's Date:

Today's Date:

Today's Date:

Today's Date:

Today's Date:

Today's Date:

Today's Date:

Today's Date:

Today's Date:

Made in the USA
Las Vegas, NV
17 December 2024

14567355R00166